VERA B. WILLIAM

The Great Watermelon Birthday

 GREENWILLOW BOOKS / New York

Published by Greenwillow Books A Division of William Morrow & Company, Inc., 105 Madison Avenue, New York, N.Y. 10016. Printed in the U.S.A.   First Edition   1 2 3 4 5 6

Library of Congress Cataloging in Publication Data   Williams, Vera B   The great watermelon birthday.
Summary: One hundred children, each with a birthday on August 10, celebrate with a party in the park and form "The Club of 101 Children." [1. Birthdays—Fiction.   2. Parties—Fiction]   I. Title.
PZ7.W6685Gr   [E]   79-17058   ISBN 0-688-80257-5   ISBN 0-688-84257-7 lib. bdg.

FOR JENNY'S BIRTHDAY

The owners of the big Fortuna fruit market in our neighborhood were an old couple. They had many grown-up children
and grandchildren. But what they wanted more than anything
else in the world was a great-grandchild.

And they got their wish.

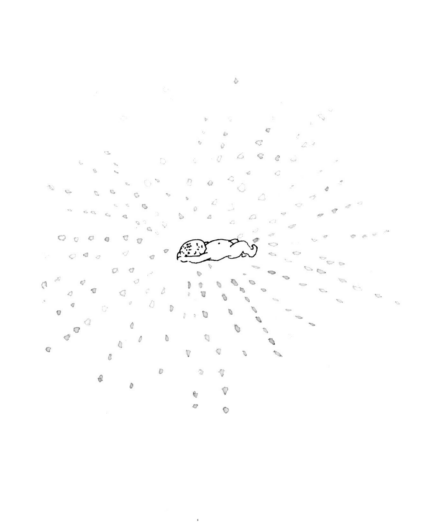

On a hot summer day one of their granddaughters gave birth to a nine-pound baby.

The mother and father named the new baby "Fortuna" in honor of the great-grandparents and the market where they had worked all their lives.

The old couple put up a big sign in the fruit market that very day.

HAPPY BIRTHDAY

OUR FIRST GREAT-GRANDBABY
WAS BORN TODAY, AUGUST 10!

IN CELEBRATION, WE WANT TO MAKE
A GIFT OF A FREE WATERMELON TO
EACH CHILD IN OUR NEIGHBORHOOD
WHO SHARES THIS BIRTHDATE WITH
OUR NEW GREAT-GRANDBABY.

PLEASE COME FOR YOUR GIFT
AROUND 5 O'CLOCK WITH A PARENT.

Fortuna Fruits

At about four-thirty that afternoon 99 children were waiting

with their parents to claim their birthday watermelons.

While they waited on line, they began to play together. Some of them already knew one another anyway. And in the end all 99 decided to meet in the park later on and have a combined birthday party. They thanked the owners of the fruit market for the watermelons and said they hoped they could come to the party with their children, grandchildren, and great-grandchild.

Just then another child came running with his mother.

Every single watermelon had already been given out,

but he left with a large honeydew melon under each arm.

He brought the number of birthday children up to 100.

And at seven o'clock that evening all 100 children with their families and friends were on the way to the park. They carried their melons and the party things they would have had at home, including two banjos, two ukuleles, and an accordion. The people who played these instruments said, "Watermelons are good—very good—on a hot night, but you can't have a real party without singing and dancing and music."

As well as the 100 birthday children there were

81 little sisters,   82 little brothers,   82 big sisters,   80 big brothers,

70 fathers,   22 stepfathers,   85 mothers,   15 stepmothers,

51 grandmothers,   42 grandfathers,   12 great-grandmothers,   8 great-grandfathers

 33 friends and neighbors,

 41 aunts,

 33 uncles,

 15 dogs,

 1 white rat,

17 second cousins,

 9 third cousins,

 8 great-aunts,

 4 cats,

 8 great-uncles,

 . . . . and 1 great-great-grandmother.

It was a real party. Altogether there were 1000 guests. They set up candles

in the cakes and watermelons and the two honeydews. Everyone shouted,

"Don't forget to wish! Now make a good wish!" All 100 children made wishes and blew

out the candles. They ate and drank and watermelon juice ran down everyone's chin.

There was some crying too. Child 31's little brother was crying. He wanted it to be his birthday too. Child 31 put some candles on a piece of watermelon. He told his little brother, "Here, make a wish. Blow out the candles. Pass it around for people to have a bite. Then it will feel like your birthday too."

Child 11's grandmother was crying. "Oh," she sobbed, "I'm so happy, so happy, so happy to be here with everyone together." Child 11 said, "Grandma, if you're so happy, you should be laughing."

That made her grandmother laugh and cry at the same time.

After that they played and hollered, talked and sang,

and danced and ran around until late at night.

At the very end of the party the children born on the tenth of August formed a club. They named it "The Club of 101 Children." The one hundred and first member was Fortuna, born that very morning and too tiny to be at the party. The members agreed that the sign of the club should be a watermelon, and they all put some of their birthday money in a jar to buy watermelon T-shirts. Their names and ages and addresses were written down by child 73 in a notebook so they could find one another again when the club needed to do something special.

Then the party ended.

Everyone started for home.

Child 99 was last to leave the park.

She was pulling her new birthday wagon

with the one watermelon that was left and her cat.

After that the park was quiet.

GOODNIGHT

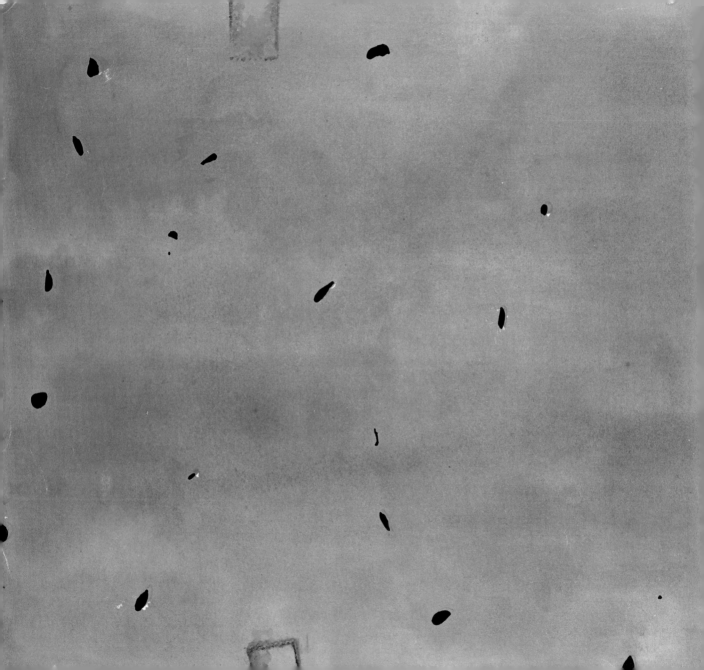